The Door is Left Ajar

里，门外

Yuki Zhang

张圣伊　著

作家出版社

昨天的你，今天的我，和明天的他

会在同一条路上相逢吗？

✦

Will your past, my present,

and their future ever mingle with each other?

目录

Contents

小荷才露尖尖角

——《门里，门外》序

　　当笔者用略带讶异的目光读完《门里，门外》这本诗集时，一时感觉有点不太真实。这真是一位少女的诗作么？它的敏感、敏锐、深刻、感伤、疑惑，明显超越了这个年龄段人所能达至的程度。只能说，这是小诗人张圣伊的天赋异禀。

　　本诗集中大多数诗，小圣伊写于新冠疫情期间。她用少女别样的明亮的审视的眼，用少女敏感的独立的清新的心，观察体悟一切。然后，用诗叙述自己对自然与社会、人生与人性、疫情与灾难、寻常与偶然、宗教与信仰、亲情与空间的诠释和哲思。其间，有尖锐的考问，有形象的比喻，有诗意的描绘，有形而上的阐发，也有一时说不清道不明的困惑。这样的认知是正常的，这样的抒

Preface

I was astonished at first as I finished reading this poetry collection. Is this really coming from a young lady who just turns seventeen this year? Her sensitivity, incisiveness, sadness, and doubts are beyond the teenagers of her age. I guess this is where her gift is.

Most of the works in this poetry book were written during the COVID-19 pandemic. Yuki observed and experienced everything with her young bright eyes and her ethereal, sensitive heart. This book provides a glance into her inner-thoughts and her comprehension of the connection between nature and society, life and humanity, epidemic and disaster, ordinariness and fortuity, religion and belief, and family and space. Writing in her own perspective, she expresses the common cognition in a colorful, poetic mood through probing questions, elaborate metaphors and descriptions, metaphysical elucidations, and a whirlwind of doubts

情是独特的，这样的诗境是多彩的。小圣伊通过自己年轻但并不稚嫩的诗句告诉人们，对世界还可以那样剖析，对人生还可以那样理解，对生活还可以那样期待。

就诗艺论，小圣伊的诗给人以美感享受。她少年式的深刻与另类，她如月光般掠过的诗思，她那种类似于刀尖上舞蹈的平衡感，她那种看似绝境却突然峰回路转的跳跃，确实与众不同。33首短诗，显示出她诗艺上的早熟与老到，也蕴藏着未来成为高光诗人的潜能。

诗，本来就属于梦想、属于青春、属于未来。对"小荷才露尖尖角"的小圣伊，亦可作如斯观。待到"映日荷花别样红"时，人们再来欣赏圣伊的诗歌，可能会忍不住慨叹：这不是当年西子湖里那朵青涩露面的小荷吗？

正是！

陈崎嵘

（中国作协原副主席）

草于庚子暮冬

of her age. In her young yet mature poems, Yuki has shown us her unique way of dissecting the world, comprehending life, and looking forward to the future.

Regarding poetic art, these works have given me great artistic enjoyment. What impresses me the most is her profound and maverick thoughts as a teenage girl—her aspiration flitting in her mind like the moonlight does in the night sky—her mind balances like dancing on the tip of knife, interchanging between desperation and hope. These 33 works have shown her mature sensitivity in poetic art and her limitless potential as a poet.

Poetry reflects one's dream, youth, and aspiration, and we can project these sentiments and expectations onto Yuki. As we read her works when she became an experienced poet, we would stop and reminisce: "Isn't she the poet whose works speak to the pandemic in 2020 back then?"

Yes, she is!

Qirong Chen
(Former vice-chairman of
China Writers Association)

答　案

妈妈跟我说，命运掌握在上帝手上

爸爸跟我说，命运掌握在自己手上

我该相信谁？

2014 年 2 月 18 日

Answer

Mom tells me

God is the master of fate

Dad tells me

We are the master of fate

Whose words exactly for me to take?

February 18, 2014

清明节

妈妈跟爸爸说

我长大了

是时候让我去南山陵园

望望爷爷奶奶了

爷爷的音容我已记不清

奶奶的最后一面也被我错过了

第一次扫墓

墓碑上镌刻的数字

对我来说只是数字

但我还是跟着念了祷告词

保佑他们在天堂幸福平安

后来的每个清明

我都跟以往一样在墓前重复着父母的话

只是多了几句没念出声的——

愿爸爸妈妈永不老去

2018 年 4 月 1 日

Tomb-Sweeping

It's time for her

To visit them

Mom tells dad

Grandpa's face long lost in memory

Grandma lives in the faintest reveries

The epitaph inscribed with words of somber

Is nothing but symbols and numbers

Paying my respects, saying my prayers out loud

I wish them merriment and laughter

With sins washed away into the gentle April wind

Yet one particular passage I keep to myself

Wish mom and dad would never be old forever

April 1, 2018

落空的祈祷

人生来自私
愿望达成时，继续虔诚地信仰着
被生活的子弹袭击时
又即刻质疑自己的信念

但那些信徒，到现在都不知
上帝答复的日子

信仰永远不会抛弃人
只有人，才可能抛弃自己

2019 年 5 月 25 日

When Prayer Doesn't Work

Human beings are born selfish

Being pious

When fulfilled their wishes

Turning their backs on Him

When being whipped by lives

Those believers haven't discovered yet

That the day when God answers

Is the moment when one believes he or she is answered

God will never abandon a believer

Only believers may abandon themselves

May 25, 2019

那所学校，那些孩子

第五年了
女生蓬乱的头发上
多了几个粉红色的小发卡
男生胸前戴歪的红领巾
也多了几滴油渍
欢畅的嬉笑打闹声
被迁移到了教学楼外新建的操场上

乌黑的眼睛里
没有落寞，没有失望
只有踏实和满足
藏在内心深处的家
不敢去想，不敢去碰
因为不知道是它先会破碎
还是自己先会受伤

The Hill

It has been five years now

The girls' disheveled hair

Are now adorned with pink hairpins

The red scarves on the boys

Are slightly askew with oil specks

And the newly built playground

Overflows with their laughter

Dark pupils

Hold no feelings of loneliness nor hopelessness

Only contentment and calmness

Too afraid to touch

The home deep in their hearts

Because no one knows

Which comes first

The collapse of the image

山上，拥抱自己五十年的银杏树

今天依旧屹立，但发现，

终于有它可以守护的东西了

2019 年 6 月 1 日

Or the ache

The fifty-years-old ginkgo tree stood in solitude

Enlivened in quietude

It finally found something worth to guard

June 1, 2019

* 在 2014 年我创立了一个专注于帮助安徽省淮北市烈山区谷山小学（一所留守儿童学校）提升教育质量和生活环境的个人专项基金，每年都会去看望那些孩子。我与这个学校的故事说来也巧合，听爸爸说，爷爷在他很小的时候给他讲过一个故事："烈山上有座庙，庙前有棵大白果树。"当初在访问安徽老家途中偶然路过了这个学校，注意到了这棵银杏树，爸爸就联想起了爷爷讲述的这段记忆。果真，我后来得知这所学校的地基就是爷爷故事里的那座庙。对学校状况了解了一番后，我决定帮助那些孩子获得更多的快乐。

* I created a charity project in 2014 that aims to help the kids by elevating the quality of education and improving their living environment in the rural area of Anhui, China, whose parents work for grueling jobs in the cities. Every summer, I visit and spend time with the kids at their school. There is an interesting story between this school and me. When my dad was a little boy, my grandfather told him about a temple up on Lieshan Hill, and a ginkgo tree stood in front of the temple. Coincidentally, I happened to notice this giant ginkgo tree, which remains there in solitude, on my trip to my father's hometown. It turned out this school has been built on the ground where the temple once stood.

不笑的三外婆

摩托车兜着我去邻里转，碾过
苗木和房子拆迁的味道
我怎么样都没想到这个村子和你，会是
我的大半个童年

烈日下弓着腰的日子没了
只剩下病房里锋利的沉默
为何我们非要在痛里找伤口
为何不在早之前紧锁的眉间领悟

那刺鼻的消毒水味
会被你眼神一瞬间的空洞压倒
你何时会再开口
何时又会再骂我

2019 年 7 月 22 日

Great Aunt

Riding pillion on the motorbike

With the smell of garden plants

And pulled-down house wood

How funny that this village and you

Make up my entire childhood

Long gone are those days you crouched under the blazing sun

Only harsh silence remained hovering over the ward

Why looking for the wound till we're in pain

Why couldn't we tell from your knitted brows

The pungent smell of disinfectant is defeated by

The dark void in your eyes

When will you talk again

When will you yell at me again

I miss your voice

July 22, 2019

* 写这首诗时是我得知三外婆直肠癌消息的第
二天。三外婆是我亲外婆的妹妹——姐妹中
的老三，从小把我带大。

* *This poem was written the day after I learned that my great aunt, who brought me up as her own granddaughter, had cancer.*

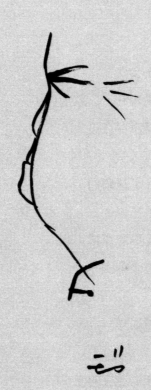

选 择

前面有一扇门
一会儿绿，一会儿蓝
当我用手去触碰它，它就消失了
也许，根本就没存在过

我用心眼推开了这扇门
眼前的一切很模糊
我被卷入了无尽的道德审判
在爱和恨的边缘徘徊
我想，或许
冷漠是更好的选择

我分不清门缝里透过的光
是救赎
还是门外伪装的人性黑洞
但我依旧期待着眷顾

Choice

There's a door in front of me

Sometimes green and sometimes blue

When I try to reach the handle, it disappears

Perhaps

The door has never been here

Everything is dim around me

Drawn into an infinite moral trial

Lingering between the edges of love and hatred

Being indifferent is a better choice,

I thought

There's light peeking through the cracks of the door

I can't tell if redemption is what it represents

Or ugly humanity in a fancy disguise

But I still eager for blessings

来自自然最纯粹的眷顾

周而复始
让所谓的"坏"，变成"好"
让人类的情感和憧憬
得以填补

也许，这门
根本就没存在过

2020 年 3 月 6 日

The purest blessings from nature

Time after time

Let the bad become the good

Let the emptiness of emotion and longing

Get to be filled

Perhaps

The door is never here

March 6, 2020

可逆化学反应

往反应物里加了点物质

平衡发生了移动

反应物增强了，产物减弱了

变成了需要的那一方

是什么快速打破了原有的状态

平衡了对他人有利的"平衡"？

是团结？是求变？

是那些几千年骨子里流淌的品质？

最终，还是选择了

雪中送炭，以德报怨

创造了新的平衡

因为它不想做一个孤独的强者

Reversible Reaction

With additional materials added

The reaction reversed

Reactant strengthens and production weakens

Henceforth,

The beneficiary becomes the benefactor

What exactly flipped the situation

Balancing the "balance" favorable to the opposite

Was it a gesture of solidarity

A pursuit of change, or

A virtue deeply ingrained

The decision is now made

Yes, repay with kindness and return with aid

A new balance is created

For the strong never wants to be lonely

我赞赏强者本能的反应:

往反应物里

加点物质

2020 年 3 月 16 日

* 对疫情期间中国援助他国的事情有感而发。

Everyone benefits, when

Adding materials

To the system

March 16, 2020

* *Thoughts on China's assistance to foreign countries during the pandemic.*

流浪者的圣经

灯红酒绿的城市里，总有某个角落

藏着背朝世界的流浪者

他们逃离孤独的人间，拒绝

扭曲的时光

夜晚是流浪者的安慰剂

他翻了个身

不用再看着牛皮公文包和华丽高跟鞋

从眼前闪过

不用再刻意拒绝这尴尬的世界

点一支烟，喝一瓶酒

他找到了充实的安逸，哪怕只在瞬间

也许，流浪者的蛇皮袋里藏着一本圣经

空虚时，读几篇旧约故事

一觉醒来后

The Vagrant and his Bible

In the corner of a neon city

There're always vagrants

Trying to evade the world

They escape from the loneliness of life, and refuse

To accept the distorted moments

Nights are his placebo

He turns over, facing back

To the leather briefcases and sumptuous high-heels

A cigarette between fingers, a bottle of liquor aside

He's eased for a brief moment

Perhaps there's a Bible in the vagrant's bag

He'd read some piece from Old Testament

Then everything will change

When he wakes up in the morning

同样的人间，就会变得不一样

他坚信上帝会答复他每天的晨祷，只是

需要点时间罢了

他相信，上帝也在流浪

偶尔，会来到他身边

2020 年 3 月 25 日

God will answer his prayers

It'd just be a matter of time

He believes that God, too, is a vagrant

Coming to his side now and then

March 25, 2020

无 题

你怕你眼中的黑

试图避开深色

但你却不知，在那漆黑的洞穴里

究竟，藏着多少宝物

等着被人发现

那片荒芜的废墟里

又有着多少顽强的小草

等着茁壮成长

2020 年 3 月 26 日

Untitled

You're scared of the darkness deep in your eyes

Trying to avoid desperately any dark side

However, you've no idea how many treasures

Hidden in these unilluminated caves

To be discovered

You've no idea how many tenacious grasses

Waiting to thrive

In that desolate waste

March 26, 2020

不挽留 = 不失去

历史告诉我
只有经历了浩劫,才会拥有自由
时间告诉我
只有放手坦然面对,才能永在路途

我们从来都不在赶路
因为不知终点在哪
所以,又何必按下暂停键,退回
就近的原点

2020 年 3 月 26 日

To Retain Is to Let Go

Famine, Pandemic, Poverty

Reprised in the whirlpool of history

Catastrophe after catastrophe

Pain after pain

Yet the fists are still clenched

Then we are truly free

I can hear the bitter laugh coming from above

The chirpy crickets and flying birds outside in the dark

Remind me of how feeble the beings inside are

The laugh will linger

Until we see through the place of misery in nature

Until we capture the patterns of time

The road keeps on stretching

Rising and sinking with changing trees alongside

And the only power we have is to proceed

The green sign shows up sporadically

But we know it never fails us

Unlocking thoughts caged by fear, regret, and questioning

I know that suffering and relief will take turns to accompany

No matter who started or ended the former

I dream about the day I become a dot in the history textbook

That page ends in uncertainty, unfinished and unresolved

But I know the next chapter is one of solace

Because we ride on that zigzag road, and always will

The ending is known

But I thought the pain we shared would unite us

March 26, 2020

梦

比妄想更可怕的
是不敢妄想
上帝给了我存在的理由
但头疼的是
我得自己寻找存在的价值

巴赫的音乐只有他本人才能听懂
对我来说，只是在毫无目的地
聆听别人的人生罢了

实际正在慢慢吞下理想
我却不想让所谓的高雅
放弃那个平凡的梦

今晚，却又做了一个
比平凡更平凡的梦

2020 年 3 月 27 日

Dream

What's worse than fantasies

Is being afraid of having one

God has given me the reason to be

But what troubles me

Is looking for the value to be

Only Bach himself can understand Toccata

A stranger's story that I'm not interested in

Reality brutally swallows up my dream

The ordinary dream I don't wanna quit

Upon the so-called elegancy

Tonight, I had another dream

Nothing but still ordinary

March 27, 2020

一万公里的思念

航班一趟趟被取消
本是带我逃离孤寂的出路
一条一条被云遮住

如今只能守着眼前这扇窗
任春夏秋冬来回更替
时间在腐化
笔纸在等待救赎

在东半球的他们还好吗？
也许爸爸脸上又多了一道皱纹
也许妈妈头上又多了一根白发
彻夜难眠的他们
是不是正在呼喊我的名字
脑海一遍遍放映着
下次相拥的场景

Ten Thousand Miles

My heart thumps each time

When I hear a flight cancel

The path of me escaping loneliness

Has been trapped in the smothery clouds

I can only gaze through the window

Through which seasons come and go

Time is withering

Feelings are eager to be jotted down

How are they doing on the other side of the world?

Years may wrinkle father's skin

Ages may gray mother's hair

Are they whispering my name

In their sleepless nights,

Over and over, picturing the scene

淅沥沥的雨

不但没带走我的牵挂

还让故乡的小路

生了锈

就如我的思念

锈迹斑斑

2020 年 3 月 28 日

When we embrace each other again?

The soft pitter-patter of rain

Has rusted the path back home

Rather than washing my nostalgia away

Just like my thoughts

Scarred and battered

March 28, 2020

乌鸦不怕雨

淅沥沥的冷雨

早已把鸟儿赶回各自的巢里

只剩一只孤零零的乌鸦

在门前草坪上觅食

爸爸说乌鸦不怕雨

因为只有在下雨天

它才能够离开黑暗的藏身之地

从陪它度过大半生的枝丫上

光明磊落地飞下来做自己

没有戒备，没有鄙夷

只是做自己

伴着冷雨，淅淅沥沥

2020 年 4 月 1 日

Crows Are Not Afraid of Rain

The little cold rain

Drives birds back to their nests

Only a lonely crow stays

Foraging on the front-yard lawn

Crows are not afraid of rain, said Dad

They only can seize the freedom

Of being themselves aboveboard

By leaving their nests under the rain

Away from the twigs on which their lifetime has spent

Neither being disdainful nor wary

Just being themselves

Under the little cold rain

April 1, 2020

不一样的窗外

春，顺着它的高枝，推开了
我的窗

忍不住想要伸手抓她
攥在手掌心里

但愿马路上的鹿和熊没看见我
不然固执的他们会以为
这又是一场人类设计的骗局
它们会以为
城市本来就是为它们设计的

大自然的生机终究征服了屋内的灰白
感谢这一年的春
让我把目光投向窗外，参与
大自然的狂欢

A Different View from the Window

Spring

Knocks against the window with her tall bare branches

Awakened from the winter's cold

A magpie comes in her elegant dark

Hopping on the red roof to search for worms

The vibrancy outside dazzles me

And the darkness inside swallows her

I'd better close the window.

Hope the bears and deer

That are taking over the street don't spot me.

They will stubbornly think of it as another evil fraud devised by

    human beings,

Even though it isn't

Now let them rule this civilized world a little longer

Like their ancestors did million years ago in this unraveled world

让我，依旧在森林里，找见

鹿和熊

2020 年 4 月 5 日

Reclaiming in their own good time.

No temperature can be felt

From the rays of early morning sun shining through the window

A static tension in the cold air insulates everything inside

Including me, having no choice but to breathe it in.

Entangled in a fog of emotions

I lock myself in stories for too long.

A leaf moving in the wind becomes a wonder

And a crow sunbathing with outstretched wings becomes a
  surprise.

They say there is a rope ladder to climb out of it

I used it, but quit after I reached for the first rung.

Indeed, salvation can be sought not only in the lines of poems
  and imaginations.

I don't want to miss the spring,

And don't want it to miss me either.

I'd better open the window now.

April 5, 2020

至少今夜我很快乐

今夜，

不是昨天的夜

不是未来的夜

就是今夜

我感到快乐

计划剩下的还是计划

弹了一会儿琴

跟妈妈视频三分钟

剩余的时间就盲目坐在这里

翻翻纸，转转笔

满是书的桌子给我好似自己很忙的假象

充实感带来喜悦

但喜悦不一定包括充实感

即使没做成什么

I'm Happy, At Least for Tonight

Tonight,

Neither last night

Nor the coming nights

Just tonight

I feel happy

Plans always to be continued

Piano I played for a while

3 minutes with my mom on FaceTime

Sitting along here watching time flies

Flipping pages and spinning pen

Faking swamped by the books to be read

A sense of fulfilment could be wellspring of joy

Joy though may not be emerged from that

Thrilled by the thought of much time ahead for me

想着今夜有大把时光任我消遣

就令人激动

5 月 22 日凌晨 00:17 的孤独

很美丽

真正属于我的孤独

很美丽

2020 年 5 月 22 日

to spend tonight

Even if nothing I've done yet

Seventeen past zero on May 22

How beautiful it is

My very moment of solitude

May 22, 2020

立场（一）

几千万个生命
在几千年的历史上
构成了一道难以抹去的轨迹
突然变道转向
只会变得支离破碎

玻璃上一旦起了雾，窗外的春天就看不清
社会中一旦起了雾，正确的思想就看不清
如果你戴着的眼镜
是用来看清眼前利益的工具
那我劝你摘下它
把目光看向历史
再去指引群众

2020 年 6 月 3 日

Stance (1)

Tens of millions of lives

Have left a track impossible to be dislodged

Mutilation will be the only way

That sudden steering lead to

You can't see spring clearly when glasses are covered by fog

You can't read the right thoughts when people emerged

   in smoke

If the glasses you are wearing

Are the tool for you to pursue selfish ends

Please take them off, then

Place your eyes upon history

And guide the crowd

June 3, 2020

立场（二）

地图正在被无限放大
"听说你们那边现在很乱"
成了近几日必收到的信息
有机可乘的新闻媒体
也开始抓住那么几个字眼
惹人们遐想某种不可能的未来

地图一旦被缩小
人，事件，时间
瞬间都变成了蚂蚁般大小
历史之河看似停滞
实则正缓缓地朝前方流淌
一个个沉重的绊脚石
被慢慢地挪开了

Stance (2)

The map is zoomed in

"What a chaos up there"

Is what they bombard me on phone

Words are taken out of context

By media opportunists

Leading people to daydream some impossible future

If the map is zoomed out

People, incidents, and time

Would become miniscule instantly

The history slowly marches forward

Though it seems immobile

The heavy blockages

are being taken out of it's way

Little by little

用放大镜看自己的不足

用缩小镜看别人的趋势

才是自强之道

2020 年 6 月 3 日

Zoom in to observe your flaws

Zoom out to perceive the tendencies of others

That's the very way to thrive

June 3, 2020

罗德岛海风

站在礁石上回味咸咸的海风
我把已被拘束三个月的自己，从诗中释放
投入
盐分恰到好处的空气中

那是自由的味道
那是治愈的味道

朝西北面看，海的轮廓很清晰
视线不再浑浊
远处的大陆收进眼底

面朝东面，才知方才的边界不是海的边界
而是海峡的边界

除了眼前无垠的大西洋，没人能理解

Rhode Island Sea Breeze

On the reef, I stand and indulge in salty sea breeze

I free myself from poems after a three-month hiatus

Diving

Into the perfectly salty air

That's the smell of freedom

That's the smell of healing

Facing northwest, the outline of the sea is clear

My vision is no longer blurred

The faraway continent comes into view

Facing east, I realize that wasn't the boundary

But the frontiers of the strait

None but the vast Atlantic before my eyes could

understand me

我的渺小

抵不过海风

抵不过波浪

不能宣泄的无助感

才是我原本的自己

唯一不变的，是我头的上方

蓝天，白云，海鸥

他们都是渺小的对应物

2020 年 6 月 5 日

My existence dwarfs compared to the mighty sea breeze

And the ferocious sea

The sense of helplessness that I can't vent

Reveals the real me

The only things won't change no matter what, are

Sky, clouds, and seagulls above my head

June 5, 2020

休止符

音乐没了休止符就不好听
人生没了休止符就不饱满
一年有大起大落
一天有小起小落
放下脚步停一停
不然你会一直错下去

即使你是对的
你也要听听休止符的悄悄话
尽管它的话没有声音

2020 年 6 月 16 日

Rest

Melody isn't beautiful without rests

Life isn't complete without rests

There are ups and downs in a year

And it's the same for every single day

Stop for a while and have some rests

Otherwise you will stay on the wrong path

Even if you are not on the wrong path

You might as well listen to the whispers of rests

Though they are soundless

June 16, 2020

随笔小记

下午 4:30

累了，休息会儿

嘀嗒……嘀嗒……嘀嗒……

叮叮咚，叮叮咚

傍晚 6:05

妈妈的一通视频电话把我吵醒了

"喂，宝贝，在干吗"

"我在写作业，先挂了"

脸换个方向

继续打盹儿

嘀嗒……嘀嗒……嘀嗒……

醒了，睁开眼，头有点晕

早晨 7:45

蓝黑笔还在手上

A Random Entry

4:30 p.m.

Exhausted, take a nap

Tick tack, tick tack, tick tack

Drrring Drrring

6:05 p.m.

A video call wakes me up

"What's going on, sweetie"

"Doing my homework. I'm hanging up"

Back to the nap

Turn my face around

Tick tack, tick tack, tick tack

Open my eyes, feeling a bit dizzy

It's 7:45 a.m.

Blue pen still in my hand

时针也还在兜圈子。

嘀，嗒，嘀，嗒……

一份有关时间与健康的作业

我写完了

2020 年 6 月 20 日

While time is still ticking away

Tick tack, tick tack, tick tack

Done

A piece of homework

About time and health

June 20, 2020

我已经很幸运了

方圆五里，或许，我站在山顶
方圆十里，必定，我沦为陪衬

雨天，或是娇媚的杜鹃
晴天，必是垂死的杜鹃

我明白了
今天的我，昨天的你，和明天的他
命运，迟早会被重叠

虽说，平凡不会被轻易接受
重要的是，当下
自己没被自己遗忘

雨天的杜鹃，依然娇媚
晴天的杜鹃，也没有死亡

2020 年 7 月 4 日

I Am More Than Lucky

Within five miles,

I may stand on the mountain top

Within ten miles,

I must degrade into a foil

Under the rain, It may be an enchanting cuckoo

In the sun, It must be a dying cuckoo

I fathom out

Sooner or later, our fates will be shuffled

Being ordinary is perfectly acceptable

It's a mature position between extraordinary and nothing

The cuckoo under the rain is still enchanting

While the one in the sun isn't yet to be dead

July 4, 2020

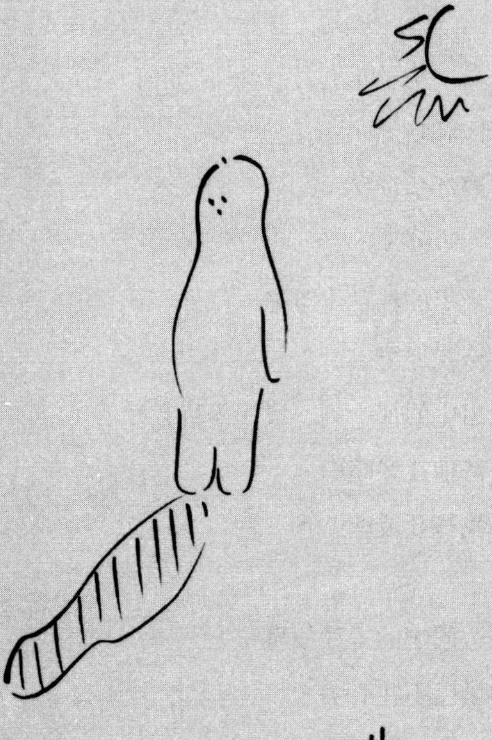

主日单

已是"庚子年五月廿六"，如何
还能呼唤
蒙着纱的记忆

余光里的红色十字架
定格在那里
从出生的那一刻，我便等待救赎
等待他在黑暗中
为我打开灵魂

耳边回响的圣经故事
却早已不在心头
过一天，勾一天
只想把时间快快推到下一个日历上

"神爱世人"这个皆知的道理

Wall Calendar

It's 26th May of Gengzi Year

How to evoke the memory

Hidden under a veil

The red cross was fixed

In the corner of my eyes

I've been waiting to be redeemed from the moment I was born

Waiting for Him to open my soul

In the darkness

The allusions ringing in ears

But not in heart

Cross off each day when it's gone

Wish time would go faster

That "God so loved the world"

突然变得好遥远

是我在这个喧嚣的世界背叛了它，还是

我从一开始就不曾抵达？

2020 年 7 月 14 日

Sounds remote all of a sudden

It's me betraying it in the bustling world or

Me having never gotten there?

                                    July 14, 2020

启示录

十六岁写的启示录

是能体会到树上的乌鸦在为你哭泣

是能感觉到神灵的力量而为你存在

邂逅世界

只需要纸、笔和一个被外界审视的生活

身体外流逝的时间不足以惜

过去，当下和未来

从不是线性结构

内心与外界之间的桥梁

我搭了很多遍

也走了很多遍

这一刻，想绽放

下一刻又会习惯性地蜷缩——

我不怕被世界抛弃

我怕，被我自己抛弃

The Revelation

The Revelation written at age 16

Is the ability to sense the crows crying for me

And the power of God flowing through me

To understand myself

All I need are a paper, pen and life examined by others

The fleeting time is nothing precious

The past, the present day, and the future

Are never linear

The bridge joining my heart and outside world

So many times I have built

So many times I have walked upon

I yearn to bloom at this moment

But flinching the next moment

Abandoned by the world is nothing dire,

Self-abandonment is the true horror

故事正被人一页页翻过去

什么时候结局渐渐不重要了

人生足矣

2020 年 7 月 30 日

The stories are being leafed through

When the ending is no longer important

Life is fulfilled

July 30, 2020

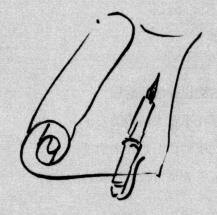

口 罩

"你没理解不怪我
怪口罩"

背后的嘴巴挣脱了封锁
提高了比平常大两倍的音量
上方的眼睛仍旧是原来的模样
不安地看着下方被左手撕烂的食指

所以
想要完全的自由
还是差那么一点点
什么时候可以轮到
我的眼睛被蒙住？

2020 年 9 月 10 日

Mask

"Not me to blame if you don't understand the words

It should be on the mask"

The mouth behind the mask free from the restraint

Raise the voice up as twice as usual

The eyes still keep the same way

Gazing the forefinger anxiously of which skin were torn

Hence

Absolute freedom

Is still one inch away

When will be my eyes' turn

To be blindfolded?

September 10, 2020

黑人小孩说⋯⋯

"对，可是"的后半句

这次依旧被吞了下去

"对，然后"成了唯一的生活方式

我清楚知晓我的透明

我也清楚知晓我在你眼中

有多么地耀眼啊

可这不是光荣的焦点

是个畸形奇怪的斑点

硬着头皮活出了别人想让我活出的样子

笑，狰狞，发怒

摆弄着各种情绪

至少让我获得了个

在社会生存的声音

The Black Kid Says...

The unfinished sentence after "yes, but"

Has been bitten back like always

The only way to live on is "yes, and"

I know how invisible to you I am

And how shining

To you I am

It's not a proud impression

But a freaky stain

Tough it out, leading the life they want for me

Hysteric, anger, distortion

Wearing emotions of all kinds on my sleeves

At least, it has given me a voice, no?

To be part of the society

可这是我吗

就当是吧。

2020 年 9 月 25 日

But…is this still the same person I used to know?

It doesn't matter if it's not,

Anyway.

September 25, 2020

顽固的一瞬间

此刻我只能麻木地

看着无数绚烂时刻从指尖流过

整理下思绪

打起精神吧！

呵

好一个打起精神吧。

意志屈服于身体

再怎么新鲜的想法

都被那疲惫的身体吞噬

高级诉说于虚空

即使堆集在记忆深处

时间也会将它消散

化为仅亮丽过瞬间的尘土

我紧张地等待下一次被绳索勒住

A Stubborn Moment

Now all I do is watch

As countless glorious moments fade

No, I cannot be like this

I must clear my thoughts

And put myself together!

Put myself together...how?

The will yields to weariness

No matter how creative the ideas are

My body gobbles' em up

Time will have' em decomposed

Into the dust that shone in a fleeting moment

Even if they're at the depth in my head

I anxiously await to be strangled again by a cord

And for the bubble to be pricked

等待有人把泡沫戳破

但此刻

我不想让兴奋打破平静的累

只想继续沉浸在这份无力感之中

2020 年 10 月 7 日

But now, just give me one moment

To indulge myself in helplessness

For I don't want the excitement

To ruin the calmness of being tired

October 7, 2020

一通电话

"考试怎么样"

"还好"

"什么，不好啊"

"还好"

"告诉我，是不是不好"

"还好"

"为什么听起来不高兴"

"没有不高兴"

"总体感觉怎么样"

"不知道"

"那估计肯定没考好"

2020 年 10 月 13 日

A Call

"How did the exam go"

"Not bad"

"What, not so good"

"Not bad"

"Just tell me the truth, was it hard"

"Not bad"

"Why do you sound upset"

"No, I'm not"

"How do you feel, then"

"I don't know"

"Well, that sounds like you failed"

October 13, 2020

疑　惑

时常向前一步

退后两步

有时候在想

是不是这世界在故意引诱我前进

到某一刻再突然给我来个

猝不及防的大跟头

滚回到了起点

2020 年 10 月 22 日

Doubts

One step forward

Two steps back

Sometimes I'd wonder

If the universe is tempting me to move ahead

And then set me back by surprise

October 22, 2020

其实我⋯⋯

很坚强

很乐观

很爱笑

很孤独

很害怕

很矛盾

你第一眼

注意到的是哪个？

2020 年 11 月 5 日

I'm Actually...

Strong

Optimistic

Cheerful

Lonely

Fearful

Struggling

What do you see in me

At first sight?

November 5, 2020

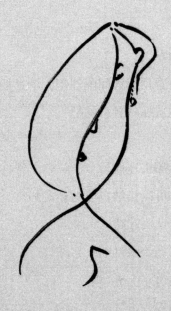

朋 友

也许真朋友

就是在与置顶那人间隔三年无消息后

还不将她从那位置移除吧

你在世界那头迷航

不断寻找可以接纳自己的新岛屿

我在世界这头迷路

不断寻找亮着绿灯的十字路口

在前行的道路上

偶尔回头看看走过的印记

心里便得到了些许安慰

可到再转向原地之时

宁愿自己从一开始就匿迹无声

告别只是为了更好地重逢

这一次我才知道

Dear Friend

What's it like to have a true friend?

It's refusing to remove her from the top of the chat list

Even after three years without messaging each other

You're getting lost on the other side in daylight

In search of your place in the world

I'm getting lost thousands of miles away in the night

In search of a crossroad where green lights are lit

I look back, now and then, at those footprints

On the path I've walked upon

Some comfort may come to heart

But returning back to the origin

I'd hope I left nothing for us to seek at the start

Now we see each other

I fight to move on

原来我们

从未放下过记忆里的彼此啊

2020 年 12 月 27 日

Until I realize that both of us

Have been holding on to this old connection

December 27, 2020

脱胎换骨

脱胎换骨始于混乱中
也许凤凰涅槃
也许真的就此零散成骨……

头高昂着
视嘲笑、谩骂为嫉妒
出生以来
如此强烈的自豪感
竟不是因为个人功绩
庆幸自己出生在
对的年代、对的地方
照照镜子
感觉脸都变漂亮许多

心却有一丝紧绷
何为危机感

Reborn

Reborn takes place in chaos

Though one may be a phoenix rising from the ashes

The other may be a speck of dust gone with the wind

No longer cares about jeers and condemnation

Because I take them as jealousy

Since the moment being taken to this world

Such pride has never been experienced

The pride not for what have been done

But for the right timing and birthplace

Even the person in the mirror appears much prettier

The heart still aches, though

What is anxiety?

How does collapse feel?

Till one can keep this sense of superiority?

何为衰落感

眼前的优越到底还能持续多久

事态加速是好是坏

我都不清楚

此刻的我

既骄傲

又好不安

2021 年 1 月 2 日

The future ahead is unknown

Whether it's good or bad that the status quo persists

Proud, as I, intranquil.

                                            January 2, 2021

比起快乐，我更喜欢忧伤

我喜欢李斯特安慰曲

不喜欢莫扎特奏鸣曲

因为我更能懂前者

我喜欢夜晚的月亮

不喜欢早晨的太阳

因为比起照亮

我更喜欢被守护

我喜欢催泪的电影

不喜欢喜剧

因为前者每看一遍都会哭

后者只有第一遍才会笑

夜深了，在月光下

I Prefer Sadness over Happiness

I prefer Liszt Consolations

Over Mozart Sonatas

For I relate better to the former

I prefer the moon in the night sky

Over the morning sunshine

For I enjoy being protected

Over being shone

I prefer sad movies

Over comedies

For I cry every time for the former

But only laugh in the first viewing for the latter

Under the night sky, beneath the moon

弹着安慰曲第三首的我

才是喜剧人物的真实写照

2021 年 1 月 5 日

Playing Liszt Consolation No.3 like I do

Is the true reflection of a comedian

January 5, 2021

节　日

有一天

圣诞节和生日

变得不再有意义

因为那个人觉得没有意义

因为她不兴奋了，不期待了

因为她对日期不敏感了

因为顾虑的事变多了

因为周围的人变了

因为她的世界更宽了

因为她不取悦自己了

因为她不相信许愿了

因为她长大了

2020 年 12 月 24 日

Holidays

There will be a day

When Christmas and Birthday

No longer matter

For they evoke no emotions of her

For they fail to generate excitement and invoke expectation

For the dates on the calendar cease to hold meaning

For concerns have occupied her mind

For people around her have changed

For her horizon has broadened

For she stops entertaining herself

For she no longer believes in making wishes

For she is all grown up

December 24, 2020

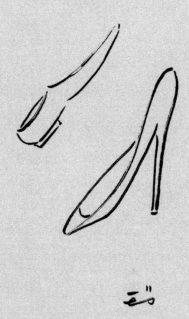

图书在版编目（CIP）数据

门里，门外 / 张圣伊著 . -- 北京：作家出版社，
2021.5

ISBN 978 – 7 – 5212 – 1376 – 8

Ⅰ.①门… Ⅱ.①张… Ⅲ.①诗集 – 中国 – 当代
Ⅳ.①I227

中国版本图书馆 CIP 数据核字（2021）第 049964 号

门里，门外

作　　者：	张圣伊	
责任编辑：	李亚梓	
封面设计：	张怡宁	
出版发行：	作家出版社有限公司	
社　　址：	北京农展馆南里 10 号	邮　编：100125
电话传真：	86 – 10 – 65067186（发行中心及邮购部）	
	86 – 10 – 65004079（总编室）	

E – mail: zuojia@zuojia.net.cn
http://www.zuojiachubanshe.com

印　　刷：	北京玺诚印务有限公司	
成品尺寸：	130 × 185	
字　　数：	58 千	
印　　张：	4.875	
版　　次：	2021 年 5 月第 1 版	
印　　次：	2021 年 5 月第 1 次印刷	
ISBN	978 – 7 – 5212 – 1376 – 8	
定　　价：	45.00 元	